This book has been written in memory of
all of the loved ones we have lost

In the quaint town of Willowbrook, under the soft glow of twilight, lived Rosieanna and her little brother Hugo.

Rosieanna, with her straight, blonde hair, loved to draw and tell stories.

Hugo, a boy with bright, curious eyes, loved to build and invent things, just like their dad used to.

Behind their cozy house was a secret garden, a magical place their dad had shown them, filled with twinkling flowers and whispering trees. Here, Rosieanna and Hugo felt close to their dad, who had passed away but left them with beautiful memories.

One evening, as stars began to dot the sky, Rosieanna said, "Hugo, do you think Dad can see us from up there?" Hugo looked up, his eyes reflecting the starlight, and nodded.

They decided to plant a special flower in the garden in memory of their dad. "It will be our star flower," Rosieanna declared, "a piece of Dad's love, always blooming for us."

Each day, they cared for the star flower, watering it with love and sharing stories about their dad. As the flower grew, so did their feeling that Dad was still with them, in every petal and leaf.

Rosieanna often drew pictures of the garden, the star flower, and of their dad, surrounded by stars.

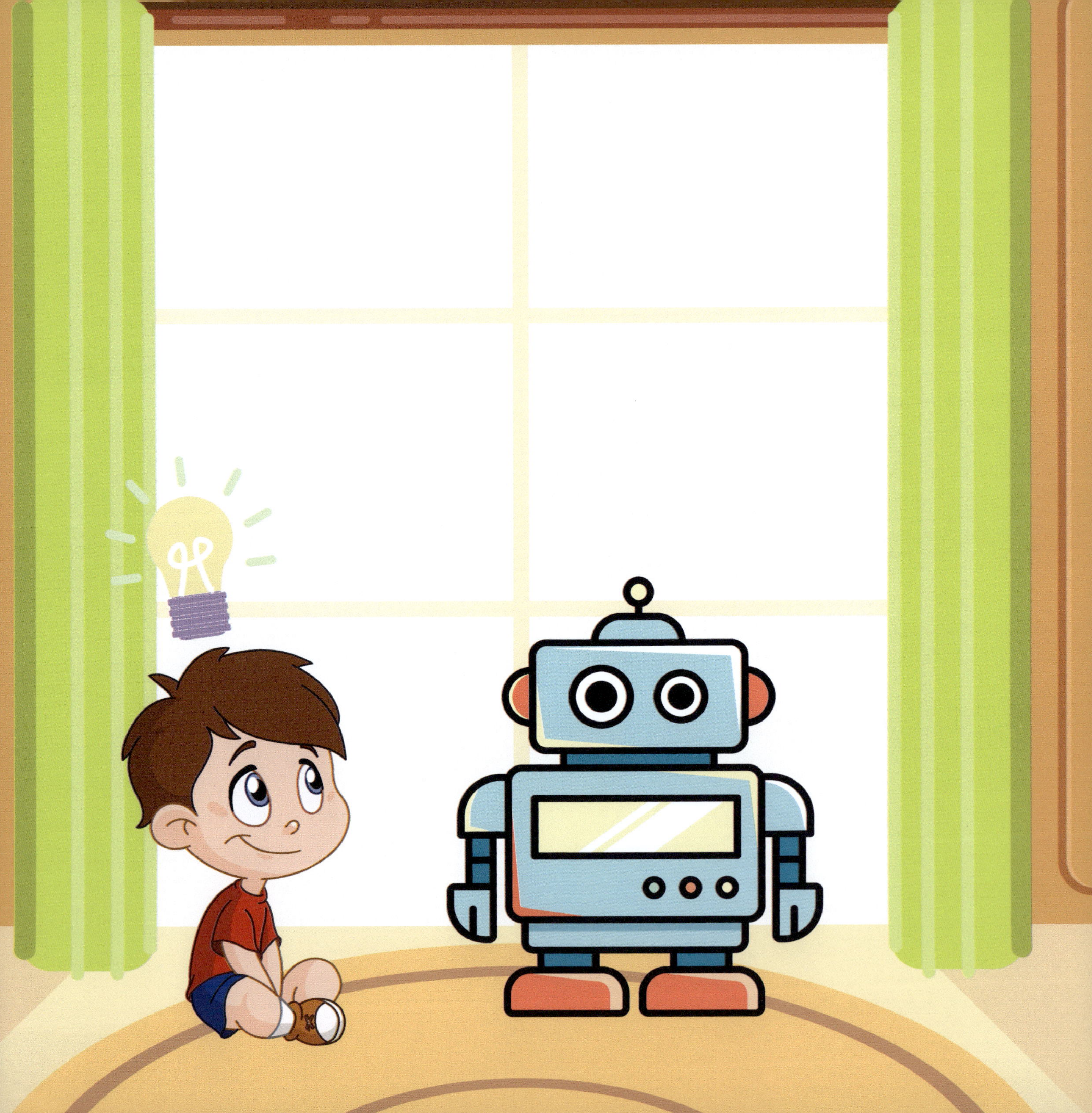

Hugo built little gadgets and inventions, inspired by the memories of their dad's clever hands.

One night, the star flower shimmered unusually bright. Rosieanna and Hugo felt a warm, gentle presence, like a hug. "It's Dad," whispered Rosieanna, "He's here with us."

With each passing day, Rosieanna and Hugo found joy and comfort in the garden. They realized that their dad's love was like the stars – always there, even when not seen.

The garden became a place of laughter, dreams, and memories, a space where they could feel their dad's guidance and watch his legacy grow in each bloom and butterfly.

Im Always With you

Whenever they missed their dad, they would visit the starlit garden, feeling the peace and love that seemed to whisper through the leaves, "I am always with you."

Rosieanna and Hugo learned that those we love never truly leave us. They live on in our hearts, in the stories we share, and in the beauty of the world they loved. Just like their dad, who continued to inspire and guide them, always a part of their starlit garden.

The End.

This book is dedicated to all those who have lost a loved one. May you find comfort in the memories, the love that remains, and the beauty they left in your heart. Remember, like the stars, their light never fades.

This book was written, illustrated and
published by Jack Harmer